Blossoms in the Desert

Debby L Wynkoop

Blossoms in the Desert

Debby L Wynkoop

This book is a work of fiction. Names, characters, places, and incidents are the product of the author's imagination or are used fictitiously. Any resemblance to actual events, locales, persons, living or dead, is coincidental.

Published by Debby L Wynkoop
DebbyLWynkoop@gmail.com

Edited by JoEllen Claypool

Cover Designed by Krista Hamel. All rights reserved.

Printed in the United States of America
April 2020

Holy Bible Scripture quotations were paraphrased from Malachi 4:2 and I Peter 5:7

ISBN: 978-1-734-7755-0-1
LCCN: 2020907343

DEDICATION

To those who faced hardship with grace and beauty.
From you we have much to learn.

Debby L Wynkoop

CONTENTS

ACKNOWLEDGMENTS

When I was very young, my family attended church with a woman who had been at Minidoka Relocation Camp. We called her Sister Koto. By the account of my eldest sibling, she was "just the most kind, sweet lady." In my distant memory, there is an image of her smiling face. She was the inspiration for the character, Misaki.

It is a wonderful thing to live in community. I am grateful to those who walked with me as this project took shape. Through their insights and input, my writing group peers and hiking partners helped me grow this story. In sharing her love of Japanese culture, Darlene Johnson provided key understandings. My pew buddy, June Tuckness, gave encouragement each week. April Johnson, dear daughter-in-law, taught me important things about the art of writing. Finally, my sweet husband, Dave Johnson, who believed in Lizzy and me all along the way.

Debby L Wynkoop

PROLOGUE

The two sisters were walking down the country road. They shared words about their day. Words they had saved just for each other. Sometimes they would say the same thing at the same time, and they would giggle.

School had let out for Easter vacation and they had plans for their free time. There was a calf that needed feeding and a ditch just filled with water to explore. There were games of catch to play and a tree to climb.

The sky was deep blue. A few clouds drifted slowly overhead. The weeks of wind had paused for a moment of quiet. Though they did not carefully look, they sensed the changes taking place around them. Sagebrush and greasewood were coming to life. Green grasses framed outcroppings of lava rock. Dots of purple and yellow spread across the rangeland. Rain from spring storms had brought the wildflowers.

They stopped next to a puddle on the side of the road. Cautiously at first, they splashed the water with their feet. The splashes grew with their laughter until they remembered their matching saddle shoes, so the girls continued on their way.

Following the curve of the road toward home, they began to skip. If they hurried, they could change out of their school clothes and have time to play before supper.

Neither girl heard it. The squealing of dusty brakes. The spraying of gravel. The thud of metal meeting flesh. Elizabeth Farris was sent into the air, landing hard in a clump of sagebrush.

CHAPTER ONE

The blue Plymouth station wagon pulled up in front of the house. It lurched to a stop. The older kids scrambled out of the car with energy saved up during the three-hour drive across the desert plain. The youngest child sat still and closed her eyes. She worried that pain might come. Cautiously she turned her head to look out the side window. Her blue eyes wide open now.

The house was hiding behind the skeleton of a tree. Brick, not wood. Pink trim. Pink trim that framed a large window. Pink trim that accented the unknown. *Blink*, she told herself.

Her mother opened the car door.

She heard the thrum of a football being caught and her brothers' shouts from across the yard. Mother reached out her hand and she took it. She pivoted her hips and used her other hand to guide the stubborn leg out of the car door. She stood, pausing to secure her balance.

Together they made their way across the lawn, scuffing through fallen leaves. They paused for a rest next to the tree, the breeze cooling her cheeks. She lifted her eyes to look at its limbs. It was just right for climbing. Then she looked again at the house.

Under the big window were bushes with crumpled leaves. *Dead*, she thought.

The game of catch had turned into a game of keep away. Her older brothers threw perfect spirals to each other as the younger two ran around trying to snatch the football out of the air.

"Boys, you have ten minutes to play, and then we'll start unloading the truck," her father called out.

Willing her leg to move, she concentrated on making the porch grow closer. When they finally reached the steps, she grasped onto the rail. Right leg first. Step and lift. Step and lift. Two more to go. With her mother's arm around her waist, and with soft whispers of encouragement, she reached the threshold. As they entered the house, the noise from the yard began to mute.

"Just a few more steps, Lizzy," Mother said. "You can do it." They moved across the living room and then down the hall. One, two, three … ten steps.

"This will be your room," Mother said while pushing the door open wide. Leaning against the frame, she could feel her mother's hands as they smoothed her blonde hair away from her face.

Elizabeth surveyed the room. Bare wood floor. Two windows. And there across the room was a bed. One, not two. She recognized her green gingham quilt and Buddy Bear. She made her way across the room. Seven steps. Turning slowly, she braced the edge of the bed with her hands and sat down. Mother backed up and gently closed the door.

In the quiet, Lizzy looked more closely. A cobweb hung in the corner. Above a metal vent, black soot stained the wall in the shape of a fan. The closet was across the room. She could make out a face in the pattern of its wood grain. Another door was above the closet door. It was the same width but shorter. She wondered what was behind it.

There were so many things missing. She closed her eyes, trying to remember. If she could picture the old bedroom with its bunk beds, then maybe she would feel its comfort.

Her thoughts were interrupted. Was someone in the room with her? Could it be?

She opened her eyes in expectation, but all she saw was the wall. The wall covered with wallpaper. Wallpaper made up of big, dusty-pink roses.

"Trespasser," it accused.

CHAPTER TWO

"Hey, it's time to eat!" Steven exclaimed as he opened the door and stuck his head into the room. "Guess I'm the lucky one who gets to escort you to supper!"

Elizabeth slowly turned to face him. In a few quick steps, he was across the room. Her oldest brother had spent a lot of time by her bedside. He read stories using funny voices for the characters. He made up games for doing ordinary things. And she liked that they shared the same blonde hair and blue eyes. She sat up and worked her leg over the edge of the bed.

"Lizzy? Are you feeling okay?" Steven's eyebrows raised in concern.

She shrugged her shoulders.

"Well, if you don't know, we'll just think everything's fine. Get your ticket ready 'cause potato soup is our destination." Steven bent his knees deeply and readied his hands. "All aboard!"

Forgetting her worries of pain, she locked her arms around his neck. Her brother held tightly to her right leg while gently keeping her left in place. Rising up, the pair made their way to the other side of the house, avoiding stacks of boxes and unplaced items.

Lizzy wanted to make the sounds of the train like Steven was doing, but her voice refused to work.

When they arrived at the doorway to the kitchen, Steven bent down again and helped his passenger get stabilized on her feet. He pulled out a stool and motioned for Elizabeth to sit. "There you go, madam. Thank you for traveling with us today."

The rest of the family had squeezed around the metal table. Elbows touching elbows. Mother was at the stove, ladling soup into bowls to be passed around.

Father's voice brought order. "Let's pray. Thank You, Lord, for this food and for Your grace and mercy. Amen."

Over the slurps and clanks of quickly eaten soup, Father spoke. "These past six months have been very difficult." He paused. Spoons slowed down. "We have shared a great loss and have needed to make many changes. With this move to Boise, we have a chance for a new start." Then the announcement came. "Tomorrow we will be going to register each of you for school." He looked at Elizabeth when he spoke. "Your mother and I think it best that you all return to your studies right away."

Lizzy was stunned by Father's words. Her head filled with dizzying thoughts, drowning out the protests of her brothers. Ever since the Bad Day, she had not considered the outside world. She hadn't thought she would go to school again.

After Lizzy was tucked into her bed that night, she lay awake thinking. She saw herself playing games at recess. She saw herself climbing up a big tree. She saw herself skipping down the road. She saw... Abruptly, she stopped herself. No more pretending. She just couldn't imagine how different school would be.

Across the shadows of the room, she focused on the print of a large rose. The wallpaper was old, like something in a museum. She knew this room belonged to someone else. She wondered about her name. She wondered what she looked like.

And with wonder in her head, Lizzy fell asleep.

Debby L Wynkoop

CHAPTER THREE

Morning came quickly. Boxes half unpacked and furniture that hadn't quite found its place created an obstacle course as the Farris family began their new morning routine. Mother directed the activity from the living room.

Today her voice was strong.

"Elizabeth, it's your turn in the bathroom. I'll be there in a minute to do your hair."

Lizzy carefully moved herself down the hallway, practicing using the crutch Father gave her the night before.

"Steven, take these boxes to the cupboard in Lizzy's room. It's above the closet so you'll need a step-ladder."

Footsteps echoed down the hall. There was a gentle knock on the bathroom door. Her mother called her name, pushed the door open and entered. Hands came to rest on her shoulders. "Should we braid it or put it in a pony?" Mother asked.

Lizzy looked at their reflection in the mirror—her blonde hair in contrast to her mother's brown. Her hair, long and straight. Her mother's short and teased. Mother wore a knee-length, rusty-orange dress with her glass-bead necklace and church shoes.

Today was important.

Lizzy lowered her eyes. Her mother began to stroke her shoulders. The sensation brought calm. "Let's braid it today so it will be sure to stay out of your face," Mother answered her own question.

Lizzy braced herself while her hair was brushed, soaking in the nearness.

When the long French braid was finished, Mother opened the bathroom door for Lizzy to make her way back to the bedroom.

"Boys, it's time to go! I'll be in the car," the call came from Father.

Steven rushed out of her room with the step-ladder in his hand. "Hey Lizzy, I found something really cool in the cupboard! I'll show it to you after school. See you later!"

She lifted her right hand to wave goodbye, but her brother was already gone.

The house was quiet as Elizabeth sat on the bed waiting to leave with Mother.

The high cupboard door wasn't shut completely. She started to think about what Steven had said, but the image of the face in the closet door bothered her. She turned her head to the side and stared at the rose wall, her hands clasped.

She heard a whisper, "Make the best of it, dear one." It did not scare her that the voice was not her mother's.

CHAPTER FOUR

Principal Williams led the way down the tiled hall. It was a while before he realized that he was walking too fast. He slowed and turned his head in their direction.

"You are going to like your new class, Elizabeth. Miss Simpson is a very good teacher, and you'll make new friends quickly." His eyes glanced briefly at her crutch and then to her Mother's face. "Mrs. Farris, feel free to watch from the back of the room until your daughter is settled. I assure you, though, that it will all go well. We'll make sure she is at the front of the building for you to pick up after school.

By the time they made it to the classroom door, Lizzy was exhausted. It was a long hallway and she wasn't used to the crutch. Father had told her last night that from now on, she would need to move herself. She knew it would be difficult, but she hadn't thought it would be lonely.

All of the students turned their heads when the door opened. Their faces full of curious stares. Five long rows of desks filled with too-many-to-count kids. With Mother's hand on her back and the principal leading the way, she was guided into the room. The thump, thump of her crutch echoed off the wood floor. The teacher made her way to the back of the room, still holding a piece of white chalk. Lizzy focused on the chalk. As the chalk grew closer, murmurs from the crowded classroom grew louder.

Lizzy's heart sunk.

The class was quickly quieted. Then the introductions were made. Miss Simpson knelt down and looked in her face. "Welcome to our class, Elizabeth. We are glad you are here."

Lizzy saw that the smile on the face of her new teacher continued into her eyes.

Shuffling took place as Miss Simpson gave commands for which desk would be where. When the seating was organized, Lizzy made her way to the empty desk at the back of the room nearest the coat hooks. All eyes were looking at the crutch.

Thump, thump. Thump, thump.

CHAPTER FIVE

As the students began to line up for lunch, Miss Simpson called a curly red-headed girl up to the front. After a whispered exchange, the girl crossed the room to Lizzy's desk.

"I'm s'pose to be your helper today and show ya what to do," she told Lizzy. "My name's Wendy."

The class lined up at the door in a boy line and a girl line. Wendy waited while Lizzy bent over to pick the crutch up from off the floor. With the teacher in front, the class made its way down the hall and down to the cafeteria.

By the time Elizabeth and Wendy arrived at the top of the steps, the class was almost through the food line. With trays filled, they stood on both sides of the tables waiting.

The two girls came to a stop. "Uh, oh" droned Wendy. She looked at Lizzy. "Can you go down steps?"

Lizzy did not know if she could, but she saw no other choice.

Hand on rail, crutch down, left leg step, then the right. Crutch, left, right. Crutch, left, right. Six times and then she arrived.

"God is great. God is good. Let us thank Him for our food." The class recited before sitting down to the business of eating.

"Sit here," Wendy directed. "I'll go get a tray for ya."

Lizzy looked around helplessly for a place to put her crutch as she struggled to move her leg under the table.

When Wendy returned with a filled tray, she put it in front of Lizzy. Without a word, she took the crutch from her hand and leaned it against the back wall.

Whispers filled the air. "So, what happened to you?" a boy in the middle of the table called out.

"Bobby, don't be rude! It's none of your beeswax," Wendy declared. Noises from the table came to a stop as she walked back and stood across from Lizzy.

"That's not rude. It's just curious," Bobby replied.

"She'll tell us when she wants to. Maybe she'll never want to. Then what's it to ya?" Wendy stared Bobby down.

The rest of the eyes were on Elizabeth Farris. Her eyes moved from the boy, Bobby, to the girl, Wendy, and then to her food. She tried to form words in her brain to give an answer, but none of them would connect. So, she picked up her fork and began to move the canned peas around her metal tray.

Debby L Wynkoop

CHAPTER SIX

Once inside the safety of the station wagon, Lizzy finally relaxed her muscles.

"Did you have a good day, Lizzy?" Mother asked with a bit too much eagerness.

Elizabeth managed a tired smile.

"Your teacher seems nice."

Lizzy thought of how Miss Simpson went to the library and brought books back to the classroom so she would have something to read during recess time. She was thankful for the Beverly Cleary book to keep her company.

"Your class has a lot of children in it! Did you meet any new friends today?"

Lizzy wasn't sure if the girl who was told to be her helper counted as a friend or not, but she wanted her mother to be pleased so she nodded yes.

Mother pulled out of the parking lot and onto the main road. "When we get home, you can have a snack and rest before supper. You must be tired after your big day."

Home? Lizzy wasn't exactly sure where that was.

The first thing Lizzy saw when she arrived at the room was the bookcase in the corner. Books had been neatly arranged on it. She turned to look at her mother's face.

"I thought you might want your old friends nearby."

Lizzy thumped her way across the floor. "It will take time, but we will turn this room into your very own special place."

Lizzy slid her hand across the bindings of some of the books. She wanted to pull one off the shelf to read but weariness overtook her. Making her way to the bed, she sank slowly into her quilt and cuddled Buddy Bear. She gave herself to sleep.

CHAPTER SEVEN

Hearing a knock at the door, her brain began to wake up. The door opened with a creak, and then her eyes opened too.

"I've been knocking and knocking. Boy, were you out cold! Hey, I promised to show you what I found in the cupboard. I think you're going to like it." Steven walked over to the bed, knelt down, and pulled out a box. He held it with a flourish and sang, "Ta dah!"

Wanting to have a better look, Lizzy pushed with her good leg and sat up in bed. It was wooden. The size of a shoebox. The wood grain created a curved design. Carved into the hinged lid were markings, like some kind of calligraphy, bordered by flowers.

"I peeked, and there are some very interesting things inside." Using his best British accent, Steven exclaimed, "We have a mystery to solve, Inspector!"

Steven gently placed the box on her lap. Lizzy felt the smooth wood and traced the outline of the small blossoms with her fingertips. Warmth worked its way through her arms and her legs and filled the inside of her.

"Pretty neat, huh?" Steven said softly.

Lizzy stared at the strange symbols on the lid before opening it. On top was a small book. It was covered with the same rose pattern as the walls. She took it out and thumbed through pages of handwriting. Then she held it up for Steven. But he didn't reach for it. It seemed he was waiting for something. Silence passed between them.

Letting out a breath, Steven took the book from her hands and inspected it. "This looks kind of like a diary," he said.

She began removing the other items from the box. One, two, three … eight objects, all very different from each other. Some paper. Some wood. One metal. They spread them out on the green gingham quilt as if they were pieces of a puzzle to be worked.

Steven held the small book out for her to see. "Look here on the title page."

My Remembrances of Minidoka
Misaki Sato
April 1960

Then he read aloud the paragraph underneath.

I never talked about it. None of us did. What was done was done, and spending time in the past takes away from the beauty of today. Now that I am nearing sunset, it seems I should write it down. My prayer is that it will bring understanding.

Brother and sister briefly looked at each other. Steven sat on the edge of the bed and settled against the headboard. Sharing the book, they turned the page and Steven continued.

The windshield wipers pushed the light rain away. In my head, I sang a song to their beat. It had been a wonderful time at church that morning. We were all excited to entertain the girls' young adult class for dinner later in the day. My son, Michael, turned the radio on as we made our way from town to the farm.

When we pulled up to stop at a railroad crossing, the music was interrupted by a news bulletin. While we heard the words, we could not fully understand them. Michael's knuckles began to whiten as his grip tightened on the wheel. My daughters in the back seat held their breath. I could only stare at the drizzle splashes on the windshield.

Inside the Hudson Sedan, we were frozen in time.

The country of my origin had attacked the country that was my home. The world—our world—was changed forever on that Sunday morning, December 7, 1941.

"Oh, Lizzy, this is when our country was attacked by Japan at Pearl Harbor. It's what brought

America into World War II. We learned about this in History class last year. Let's see the cover of the box again."

Lizzy closed the lid, and they looked at the symbols carved into it.

I think this is Japanese writing. I wonder what it says."

Lizzy traced the symbols with her fingertip. Steven turned back to the story.

It was the longest walk of my life. With a suitcase in each hand, we went down the road lined with barracks, looking for Block 41. My eyes blinked against the wind that stirred up the dust, stinging my arms and face. I wondered why I had worn my pink dress. Later, I would see how the dirt stole the brilliant white of the lace collar away.

Fifty-five years of life packed into two suitcases. My family a number—3,253—typed in red on tags tied around the handles.

Lizzy reached for the pasteboard tag. She stroked her thumb lightly over the numbers and the name Sato. Then she looked around the bedroom at the closet and the books and at Buddy Bear. Would everything she had fit into two suitcases?

Steven kept reading.

I tried not to think about the uniformed guards with rifles. I wanted to keep the tears from leaving my eyes, so I concentrated on the simple act of moving my legs. One step at a time.

At last we arrived. Opening the door, we entered our quarters. Tired from the train and truck and walk, tired from living in a horse stall at the fairgrounds, tired from the hurried decisions and uncertainty; I set down my suitcases.

I looked around. Wood floor. Pot-bellied stove. One light bulb hanging down. One cot pushed against the wall. And clapboard walls. Clapboard walls that let in the outside. Clapboard walls, bare and stark.

"Foreigner," I heard the accusation echo in my head.

Michael came to put an arm around my shoulder. "It's going to be okay, Mom," he said as the girls huddled next to us.

We stood in silence until I found my voice. "Shikata ga nai," I whispered. There is nothing we can do about it, so we will make the best of it.

Steven's voice paused and then he repeated, almost as if asking a question. "Make the best of it. Funny, I studied about this stuff last year, but I never thought what it was like for the people involved."

Lizzy thought about her day. Everything she had done was difficult. She had tried her best, but she did not think it would ever be okay.

Debby L Wynkoop

CHAPTER EIGHT

Brother and sister continued reading the story.

The heat on that August day was smothering. I had always lived in green places. Places where rain was a partner in growing vegetables and flowers, where the air was sweet and easy to breathe, and where the skin was kept soft. Here was a brown place.

Michael and the girls went out to search for anything that might make the first night in our quarters more bearable. I knew my adult children were resourceful and I was blessed to be with them. Other Issei were not as fortunate.

They went to the mess hall to eat supper. Mess hall. What an odd name! Gone were the comforts of our dining traditions. On that first day in camp, I could not bring myself to eat food someone else had prepared. Noises from the apartments next to ours came in over the partitions. Bathrooms and showers in the open to share with people I did not know. Too much strangeness.

I walked out the door and down the block to a little hill nearby, where the ground was not torn up by the machinery used to build our city in the desert. Sagebrush and black lava rock surrounded me. In the distance, through the haze, I could make out the profile of mountains. Not too far away was a river. A large canal, I was to learn later.

Even though the guard in the nearest tower could see me, I no longer cared. I sat *on the ground. My pink dress mattered no more. I stared at the moving water and poured my heart out through my eyes.*

When my sob quieted, I listened. I could hear bird call and the rustle of brush in the breeze. And I could hear Him say, "Here I Am."

Steven's voice had grown soft. "Let's stop there for now," he said, interrupting her thoughts. "It's close to supper time, but I think we can finish reading it tonight."

Together they returned the items to the box. Steven marked the spot in the story with a gum wrapper from his pocket, and they put the book on top.

"I think this belonged to the woman who lived here before us. Her family will want it, but for now let's keep it our little secret."

During supper, her three younger brothers did all the talking. They rushed to get words out about their first day of school. Mother reminded them to not talk with their mouths full of food. Steven was quiet through the meal, eating quickly. He was the first one to be excused.

Later, he returned to Lizzy's room to finish reading the little book.

My body awakened the next morning with the desire for more sleep. It had been a restless night on the army cot. But this would be the day for a new start. I would work to make it productive, to make it go by swiftly.

Putting on a house dress and sturdy shoes, I walked to the mess hall with my children. Inside were groups of Issei men and women sitting at separate tables. Clusters of young adults and school kids huddled together. We got our bowls of oatmeal and went separate ways—the girls to a table of young women and Michael to a group of Nisei men. Looking around, I found a place to sit with some older ladies. It was there that I met Ichiko.

After eating, the hall fell into an uneasy silence. The people sat, uncertain as what to do next. In that pause, voices at Michael's table stirred and grew louder until anger bit at the air. When the anger was pushed back down, we stood as one people. We would go out and make for ourselves a home in the middle of the desolation.

Silence. Anger. Desolation. Lizzy knew these words, but she did not like to think about them.

They read the rest of the memoire, matching each item from the box to what was described. When they finished, they sat still for a while. Then they returned everything to the box the way they found it.

"Let's keep it under the bed for now." Steven said. As he left the room, he mustered up his best pirate voice. "We have found the buried treasure, aye matey?"

When Mother came in for evening prayers, Lizzy wanted to tell her about the special box and its book. She was sure she could make the words come out. But wanting the secret more, she kept her voice quiet.

"Lord, thank You for this day—for keeping us safe and for giving us strength. Thank You for a new beginning," her mother prayed. The kiss lingered on Lizzy's forehead as her mother turned off the light and closed the door.

The memory box under the bed filled the room.

CHAPTER NINE

Lizzy walked out of the school building, crutch in one hand and the paper plate skeleton in the other. She spotted the station wagon near the front door. The first week Mother had helped her, but this week Lizzy was left by herself to get into the car.

There were more cars in the lot today. Kids hurried all around her like wind-blown leaves. Leaning on the crutch, she tucked the skeleton under her arm and opened the passenger door.

Wendy, with her little brother dressed as a hobo, passed by on the sidewalk. "Happy Halloween, Liz!" she called out.

"How was your day?" Mother asked as Lizzy got settled.

Each day she was asked that same question.

"What do you have there?"

Lizzy held the skeleton to show her mother the work she'd done in science class. The skeleton was held together with small brass brads, and each bone was carefully labeled.

"Very nice work, Lizzy. What an interesting project!"

Lizzy smiled at the praise. She wanted to tell her mom that the skeleton's name was John, but she decided that detail was unimportant.

The house was quiet when they arrived. Father would not be home from work until supper time. Her brothers were always busy with school activities. Steven had begun working at the Taco Shack a few hours each evening and sometimes he even missed supper.

Lizzy found her snack on the kitchen table. The cupcake from the class party had filled her up, but she was happy to see a small brown paper sack with pumpkins and a scarecrow drawn on it. Inside, she found a mix of her favorite candies.

Before laying down for her nap, she read from Misaki's memoire, the books on the shelf ignored. Steven had said that he told Father about finding the memory box. Misaki's son would come to pick it up next summer, but until then, she was allowed to keep it in the room with her.

The box kept her company. Especially on this night when other kids were out trick or treating.

Debby L Wynkoop

CHAPTER TEN

From her desk in the back of the room, Elizabeth looked at her teacher. The bulletin board was crowded with turkeys. Turkeys made from cut outs of hand prints—orange, red, and brown. Cartoon pilgrims marked days on the calendar.

While the sky outside was gray, she found sunshine in Miss Simpson's voice. "Class, you have really been working hard," Miss Simpson began. "Today is Friday, and I think it is a good time to do an activity. This project will give us something cheery to display in our classroom."

Lizzy looked at the large piece of construction paper. It was as big as her desktop. It had been cut into the shape of a puzzle piece.

Miss Simpson instructed, "We are going to make a class mural. A mural is a piece of artwork that fills the space of a wall. All of our separate pieces will fit together, and we will call it 'Happiness Is'. I want you to draw a picture to answer the question, 'What makes you happy?' Use all of the space on your paper for drawing. After your sketch is finished, outline it with a dark crayon. The final step will be to paint with the watercolors and lay it out to dry on the back table."

Lizzy sat unmoving.

She heard Bobby declare in an everyone-can-hear-you-anyway whisper, "Candy! Candy! Candy! I'm gonna draw all my favorites!"

Wendy leaned over. "That Bobby, he's not exactly a deep thinker, now is he?"

Lizzy smiled at her friend's bluntness. "I'm thinkin' about drawin' my dog, Waffles. He makes me happy. What are you gonna draw, Lizzy?"

Lizzy shrugged her shoulders.

"Not sure yet, huh? It will come to you." Wendy turned to begin her work.

Lizzy was glad that her friend did the talking for both of them.

Closing her eyes, she tried to remember. Happy had been a long time ago. Her classmates were busy at work, so she picked up her pencil. Her grip tightened as she struggled to find an idea. Next to her, Wendy was humming as she drew. Recognizing the tune, her mind began to sing. It was a song they were learning during music time for Thanksgiving. "For the beauty of the earth ..."

The muscles in her hand relaxed. Setting the pencil to the paper, she started to work. Lines, curved and straight, blended together. First the big shapes. Then the details. To Elizabeth's amazement, she had drawn a picture of her happiness.

Wendy put the finishing touches on her Waffles picture. She glanced sideways.

"Oh, jeepers, Liz! That's great!"

Miss Simpson looked their direction and slowly walked to the back of the classroom. With a gentle hand on Lizzy's shoulder, she bent over to look.

In the middle of the paper was a large tree. Big limbs. Each limb with branches. Each branch with leaves. Sitting on the biggest limb was a smiling girl with legs dangling down. And on the limb above, hidden a bit by branches and leaves, was another girl. A girl with the same blouse and the same blonde hair.

CHAPTER ELEVEN

Saturday morning cartoons were on the television. Lizzy's favorite was Bugs Bunny because Steven could always do the perfect eh-what's-up-doc voice. When her brothers changed the channel to watch Flash Gordon, she decided to go back to her room. Looking into the box, she pulled out the rose. Pressed and dried and faded. She carefully set it on the night stand. Then opening the little book to just the right spot she began to read.

The fall came, bringing relief from heat. Schools for the children and youth had started. Churches began to meet. Jobs were assigned. Facilities improved. Furniture made. Life began to flow in a kind of rhythm.

But the river dried up.

Taking the pink rose in my hand, I studied it—glad I had cut it from my garden before the chaos came. I had taken great care to dry it and keep it with me, for I knew I would not return to my Oregon home. Staring at the bare wall of our living quarters, I knew what I should do.

There is the beauty that God made. There is beauty that people create.

It was late autumn before the supplies, ordered from Sears and Roebuck, finally arrived. The War had brought shortages and slowness. Michael delivered the package to me when he returned from the post office near the main gate. It had been opened and inspected before being rewrapped and released. He presented it as I sat with my Issei friends in the mess hall. Each day, things arrived on the block that brought a ripple of interest. It became a game to guess *what was inside. It was a reminder of the world outside.*

While I had told no one of my plan, I was happy to share the excitement. I slowly unwrapped the package and displayed the items on the table. Murmurs of approval rose from the group. I would begin the project the next day.

Lizzy reached over and took Misaki's art brush out of the memory box. She stroked her left leg with its soft bristles before reading the next part.

I have always been thankful for the name my parents gave me: Misaki, Beautiful Bloom. Blossoms come after winter days are over. No matter the sorrow in my life, joy has always followed. Sadness of leaving Japan was followed by joy of a new life. Grief given to me by the accident that took my husband's life was followed by hope that grew with my children. People want to run away from what makes them sad, but without sad, we could not fly to the happy.

One of happiest days of my life was when I finished the mural. Putting away the remaining paint and brushes, I sat in the middle of the small apartment to meditate and pray. Though I could feel the cold air swirling around my body, my mind traveled to another place. Sakura—a flowering cherry tree. Green hills. Blooming rose bush. Flowing stream. The naked wall had come to life.

On Monday, the students shuffled into the classroom. Excitement broke out when they saw the mural on the wall. Elizabeth entered the room last, just behind a cluster of girls. She stopped her crutch and looked up. All of the artwork was fit together in a colorful display. Her precious tree was in the middle.

Awkwardness grabbed at her. Hurrying through the morning routine, she closed her hearing to the sounds around her.

The board work read, 'Write a paragraph to describe your artwork.'

Lizzy wrote, "Happiness is a tree. Happiness is climbing a tree. Happiness is a left leg that works. Happiness was before the Bad Day."

CHAPTER TWELVE

Dark enfolded the days of December. Turkeys on the bulletin board were replaced by red and white Santas in varying shapes and sizes. Stockings replaced pilgrims on the calendar. But the mural of happiness still filled the wall.

Lizzy had grown weary of reading every recess. She liked her latest library book, *A Wrinkle in Time*, but she longed to be with her classmates outside. Setting down the book, she listened as the pounding feet in the hallway grew closer. The excited voices made her wonder what she had missed.

After the coats were hung and drinks at the fountain finished, Miss Simpson addressed her students. "Class, this afternoon we will have our final practice for tonight's Christmas concert. It will be a dress rehearsal. That doesn't mean we're wearing our concert clothes. You'll do that tonight. It means that we will go through all of the songs and narration in order and without stopping. I expect each one of you to be on your best behavior and to work hard."

The students filed into the cafeteria-turned-auditorium. Going down the six steps was getting easier. While the class crowded onto the risers, she took her place next to Wendy, but on the floor level. A chair had been positioned behind her. "Just in case you need to rest," Miss Simpson had said.

She loved the songs the teachers had chosen, but she really didn't need to sing. Wendy sang loud enough for the two of them.

At the first practice, the teacher from the classroom next door had told Lizzy that she was to open her mouth and move her lips. Instantly, Lizzy's strength left her. She sat down awkwardly on the floor, the crutch clattering on the tiles.

Unsure what happened the rest of the afternoon, she became aware that Mother was in the classroom talking with Miss Simpson and Next-Door-Teacher. Lizzy wasn't sure if she was in trouble. She didn't know what she had done wrong. She just knew she felt awful.

During first recess the following day, Next-Door-Teacher came with a drum and two drumsticks.

Miss Simpson sat in Wendy's chair and began to talk. "Elizabeth, your mother told us that you've had piano lessons. We need someone who knows their rhythms very well to play a special part on the drum. Would you like to try?"

Lizzy kept her eyes lowered as she thought. Yes, this is something she could do. She nodded.

So Next-Door-Teacher taught Elizabeth to play the drum part. It only took a few recesses to learn. She would play the drum from her place by Wendy, while Bobby would stand next to her with the big bass drum.

Now that program day had come, she was very excited. Her classmates were excited too. There was a constant buzz of noise from the risers during their last practice.

They finally came to the special song, "Little Drummer Boy". Bobby brought the mallet down on cue, and Lizzy came in with her pa-rum-pum-pum-pum rhythm. But Bobby's notes kept getting faster and faster.

Next-Door-Teacher cut them off. "Bobby Thompson, you're rushing. You must make sure to play exactly when my hand goes down on beat one."

Bobby looked at the teacher with a sheepish smile. "I'm sorry, Mrs. Morris," he said. "I guess I'm just freakin' out a bit." He glanced over his shoulder.

Snickers and giggles emerged from the risers.

"Well, take a deep breath. Listen to Elizabeth and stay with her." Then with a hint of hopelessness in her voice she added, "You must hold the beat steady."

"Bobby, you want me to take your place?" Wendy whispered from the end of the riser.

"No way, Wendy! Liz and I are hangin' tough!" Bobby winked at Lizzy, then took an exaggerated breath.

That evening, the school was crowded. With her blonde hair tied in a velvety red ribbon and wearing last year's Christmas dress, Elizabeth stood in her place. She searched the audience. Her family was lined up in the same row of folding chairs— Father, Mother, and her four brothers. Steven had asked for the night off so he could be there. "I can't wait to hear you jam on the drum," he had said.

She saw Bobby out of the corner of her eye. His hair was slicked back. He tugged at his collar trying to adjust the tie.

Wendy walked in smiling. "Oh, Liz, ain't it wonderful!" she said pointing to the giant Christmas tree full of decorations. Giving Lizzy a quick hug, she stepped up on the riser.

The concert began. With each song, happiness grew. Then it was time. Bobby took his place, sending a confident smile her direction. With mallet in hand, she could hear him take a breath. Boom, boom he played. Pa rum pum pum pum she played. The voices of her classmates joined them. And it all fit together. Perfect unity.

By the final song, Lizzy's joy had found its way to her lips. They moved in unison with her class-mates. And by the end, sound came out. "Sing we joyous altogether, Fa la la la la la la la la. Heedless of the wind and weather, Fa la la la la la la la la!"

Applause filled the hall. Lizzy looked at her family. Her brothers' hands clapping. Father's hand around Mother's shoulder. And her mother's hands wiping away tears.

CHAPTER THIRTEEN

After the concert that night, Mother served hot chocolate to the entire family.

Father would not allow them to stay up past bedtime, though. There were two more days of school before vacation.

When Lizzy settled into her room for the evening, she pulled out the little book to read.

Winter was harsh. Dark came early each day. Shortages of coal. No supply of wood. Constant wind. We filled the gaps in our walls with whatever we could find. But it was never enough. The only warmth was in family and friendship. We met to worship, volunteered at the school, shared hobbies, and told stories. We quietly talked about the War and wondered over the future.

And Ichiko became to me like a sister.

Many things were missing that first Christmas in the camp. No Christmas trees. No red. No white. We avoided those colors, for fear of appearing loyal to the Emperor of Japan. Our small congregation gathered on Christmas Eve, the Methodist pastor telling the story by candlelight. A solitary star served as decoration.

How strange to think people everywhere were celebrating the birth of Jesus, the Prince of Peace, while fighting overwhelmed the world. How strange to think that while we worshiped the Christ Child in this bleak place, our friends and neighbors from before the War gathered to worship in beautiful cathedrals and buildings.

I understood like never before what it must have been like for Mary and Joseph.

There was no room for them, except in a barn. There was no room for us, except in this barren desert.

It must have occurred to Ichiko as well. Standing next to me, she took my hand. And we sang. Kiyoshi, kono yoru. Silent night, holy night. Our voices as one. Christ the Savior is born.

On Christmas afternoon, a knock was at our door. Michael jumped up to open it. He quickly ushered my friend into our quarters, slamming the door against the wind behind her.

With a slight smile and a bit of drama, she set down her bundle and took off her coat to display a floral kimono. Then with deep bow, she stretched both hands to offer the gift. I bowed to receive it.

Opening the package with proper care, I discovered a beautifully crafted box made *of polished greasewood. It was carved with my name in kanji and cherry blossoms on the lid.*

"We must always remember," Ichiko said. "Merry Christmas."

Tucking the book back into its box and closing the lid, Elizabeth once again traced Misaki's name. Smoothness under her finger tip. It usually made her feel happy. But tonight her thoughts were troubled.

Remember.

She did not want to remember. Remembering hurt.

CHAPTER FOURTEEN

The clouds had moved in, and they all could feel it. Miss Simpson's voice drifted off. She set down the social studies book. "I surrender," she said to puzzled faces. Then smiling, she strolled to the windows and began pulling up the shades.

Bobby was the first to blurt out the obvious, "It's snowing!"

Thirty-four students rushed to the side of the room with the windows, needing to confirm for themselves what Bobby said.

Lizzy was the last to get there. Looking between the bodies of her classmates, she could see the big flakes floating down from the white sky, dancing and swirling as they fell. It was when she started to back away from the window that she realized she hadn't taken the time to pick up her crutch.

It snowed into the evening. The valley and the plateaus above were covered in a white blanket.

When Lizzy arrived at school the next day, she saw kids on the playground rolling balls of snow. On occasion, a snowball would fly through the air. Tall mounds of snow were piled up. The snow plow had already cleared the parking lot.

Slowly, Mother pulled up to the front door. "I'll help you. There may be ice," she said, putting the car in park.

"I want to play outside." Elizabeth said.

Mother looked at Lizzy, her mouth open.

"Oh, Sweetie … Lizzy. I … I'm not sure today is the day to go to the playground. There's snow and ice and cold and kids acting crazy. Why don't we wait until the New Year."

Lizzy sat unmoving. "Please," she said.

Mother closed her eyes for a moment. A tiny stream of water made its way down her cheek.

"All right. I'll drive over to the playground lot. Bundle up. Do you know where to go when the bell rings?"

Lizzy nodded yes.

Lizzy learned quickly to walk where the snow was fresh and not packed down. She moved past the basketball court.

Wendy came running toward her. "Hey, Lizzy! Come on. We're makin' a snowman!" Wendy took off to rejoin the gaggle of girls. Lizzy made her way over to them. "We wanna make it as big as we can!"

Lizzy watched for a moment. With no good place for the crutch, she set it on the snowy ground. With her mittened hands, she began to smooth the surface of the giant ball. Soon, a system was in place: some girls rolled snow over, some girls packed the snow into the ball, and others smoothed and rounded it out. And Lizzy was a part of it.

A group of older boys sauntered across the playground. "Whatcha doing?" the boy with the plaid hunting hat called out.

Wendy stood as tall as she could and answered, "What do ya think we're doin'? We're makin' the best and biggest snowman ever!"

"Is that so? How you plan to do it with that crippled girl on your team?" He pointed right at her.

Lizzy wished she could melt into the snow.

The bell rang, and the boys ran off laughing.

"Pay them no nevermind, Liz." Wendy said. The others chimed their agreement.

Surrounded by sympathy, Lizzy was escorted to the girls' line.

"Yeah, they're just a bunch of jerks. Probably jealous," Bobby said as he passed by.

CHAPTER FIFTEEN

At first recess, Lizzy put on her scarf, hat, coat, and mittens to go outside with the rest of her class.

Wendy handed her the crutch before lining up. She held it for a while, then set it down in the bottom of the coat rack.

The girls were busy at work by the time Lizzy got there. The middle section was under construction. By the end of recess, they were faced with the problem of how to get it on top of the bottom snowball.

"Boys, the next time I see a snowball flying through the air, you'll all be standing against the wall!" Next-Door-Teacher yelled, bringing the snowball fight to a sudden end.

Several boys from the class ran over. They inspected the girls' work. "How are you gonna get it up there?" one of them asked. "It's too big and heavy to lift up."

The girls didn't have a plan. They had been more concerned with making the balls big, round, and smooth.

"I have an idea," Bobby said. "Let's build a ramp like army guys do, and roll it up." And so with a useful idea, the girls let the boys in on their project.

"Who would've thought it? Bobby's smart." Wendy said to no one in particular.

By lunch recess, the middle section had been rolled up on the bottom, and the head was in place.

Miss Simpson brought out some items to add to what the kids had found: yardsticks for arms, a broom from the janitor, a scarf from the lost and found, a carrot from the lunchroom for the nose, and finally a top hat borrowed from the costume closet. Giving the class extra time, they put on the finishing touches. No one could reach the top of the snowman, so Miss Simpson lifted Lizzy up to put on the hat.

The snowman had come to life.

Lizzy's body was so tired. She wanted to lay her head on the desk and imagine things—to make up stories about the snowman. But it was math time, so she raised her hand for permission to sharpen her pencil.

Wendy looked at her a bit puzzled. She usually sharpened Lizzy's pencils for her.

Lizzy stretched her legs out and hobbled to the pencil sharpener. Glimpsing out the window to admire their snowman, she froze in disbelief.

Enough. Enough hurt.

"No!" she cried out. "Stop. Stop. Stop it!"

Every student in the class looked at her shocked.

Miss Simpson hurried across the room to the window side. Chips of snow spurted into the air as the sixth-grade boys kicked at the snowman. Plaid-Hat-Boy started pushing at the head to topple it over.

"Please. Please. Please stop!" Lizzy pled.

Grabbing her coat, but not taking time to put it on, Miss Simpson ran out of the classroom. The clank of her shoes sounded from down the hall. All of the students moved to the windows to see the drama unfold.

Lizzy closed her eyes, unable to watch the destruction.

"Oh, they're so gonna get it now," Wendy declared.

"Get 'em, Miss Simpson," Bobby called out.

"Simpson, Simpson," the boys began to chant.

The chant covered up Lizzy's moans.

The students scrambled back to their seats as Miss Simpson's steps neared the classroom door.

Lizzy stayed at the window, her head still bowed. Wendy had brought a box of Kleenex over, but Lizzy's tears were dry.

No one moved as their teacher walked to the fountain to get a drink and then approached the two girls at the window. "Lizzy, thank you for telling us that something was wrong." She gently directed the girls to their seats, and then made her way to the front of the room and sat on her stool.

Lizzy looked down at her desktop. Emptiness was all she could feel. She concentrated on the sound of the ticking clock.

"Well, our snowman has been damaged," Miss Simpson began. "I'm very sorry, for I know how hard you worked to build him."

A couple hands went up. "Yes, Bradley?"

"Are they going to get in trouble?"

"Their teacher will take care of it. They won't bother the snowman again." She gestured for the upraised hands to be lowered. Taking a deep breath, she continued, "Sometimes bad things happen. It's okay to be angry and sad. But then we have a choice to make. Either we can stay mad and sad, or we can do something to make it better." Miss Simpson paused. "What do you think?"

Elizabeth looked up. Hands all over the room were raised. A plan was made. And hope began to fill the space in her heart.

Debby L Wynkoop

CHAPTER SIXTEEN

The Farris family gathered around their small kitchen table for a spaghetti supper. Slurps of noodles sent tiny specks of red sauce through the air.

Lizzy watched the animated faces of her brothers as they told about their snow adventures. She was happy that she had her own story.

As the slurps slowed down, her parents' eyes met. Mother gave a little nod.

"Lizzy, I understand that you played out in the snow today," Father said. Her brothers looked up from their nearly empty plates. "What did you do?"

Lizzy smiled, her brothers suddenly quiet. Yes, this was something she could do.

"Today, my class made a snowman. A really big snowman!" she began. "He had a great big body and a carrot nose. He had arms and was holding a broom. There was a scarf around his neck. And Miss Simpson lifted me up to put a hat on top of his head. We named him Cool Kevin." Lizzy's words slowed down. "Then the big kids came and tried to knock him over, but Miss Simpson stopped them. Our class went back outside and fixed him up," she continued. "We built a fence out of snow and a snow dog to stand guard. Then Wendy made a sign that said, 'Beware of Dog.' We didn't even have to finish our math today. It was so much fun!"

After she finished, her brothers cheered and laughed. Steven patted her back. And her parents smiled.

She had told them all about it. Well, mostly. She didn't talk about the bully. Or the name calling. It was hard for her to think about bad things. But Misaki told both good and bad in her story. Without sad we could not fly to the happy, Lizzy remembered.

After supper, Lizzy decided to read the sad part again.

Two days after Christmas it came—suddenly, with no warning. On tip-toe I looked out the small window. Instead of falling to the ground, this snow traveled sideways.

Ichiko's husband had snuck out the main gate earlier in the afternoon to look for greasewood. He had begun a new project and needed just one more perfect piece.

We did not know until the next day that he had not returned. They found his body, frozen, curled up against a lava rock ledge.

We could not win the battle with the cold.

Lizzy touched her cheek. And felt a tear.

Debby L Wynkoop

CHAPTER SEVENTEEN

Elizabeth sat with her classmates in the cafeteria-turned-gymnasium. She was just beginning to feel her fingers and toes again. She did not like how they stung. She stretched her left leg out, but it burned with ache.

The students had been rescued from the cold that morning by Principal Williams. He opened the hall doors and called for them to come off the playground.

Now Lizzy waited to be rescued by Miss Simpson. Rescued from the noise and the crowd and the nothing to do. And from Plaid-Hat-Boy who she could see across the room.

"Hey, Liz." Bobby said as he walked her way. His beet-red nose made him look like a leftover Santa. "It's so cold outside, my snot froze," he announced to the whole class. "I keep sniffing but nothing is moving." Bobby inhaled dramatically through his nostrils before sitting down next to her.

Lizzy's face felt a sudden warmth. A warmth that came from inside herself.

Laughing, Wendy squeezed into a space next to Lizzy. "Geez, Bobby. How much ya got in there, anyway?"

Miss Simpson arrived to line up the class. It took extra effort for Lizzy to stand back up, and she wobbled to get her balance. From across the room, Plaid-Hat-Boy pointed. Guffaws bounced off the wall to her ears.

Wendy reached out to steady her.

"Thanks. I'm good now," Lizzy whispered, aware of the sixth-graders' eyes watching. "I can walk by myself."

"I'll help ya up the steps," Wendy said as they moved in the line.

Lizzy stopped. Her friend grabbed onto her arm, but she pushed it away.

Wendy rocked back on her feet.

Lizzy hobbled up the steps. Alone.

She could feel the blast of hot air from the heat register as she entered the classroom. She could feel the cold from her friend.

"Class, I think it's a good day to get our room ready for February. With the temperatures below zero, we will probably be inside for recesses. There are a few minutes before school starts. Let's begin by taking down all of the January artwork and the Mural of Happiness. You can take those things home today."

The students went to work. Lizzy sat at her desk, sad that the pain had returned. When her precious tree was placed on her desk, water came to her eyes. She sensed some classmates gathered around her.

"Lizzy," Bobby began, "Your artwork sure is great! I can see you in the tree," he said while pointing. "But we've all been wondering ... who is this other girl?"

Panic replaced the pain. She could not think. She would not remember. Building a fence around herself, she kept silent.

Later that evening, Steven came to her room before bedtime. He had the night off work. Not too many people buying tacos during the bitter cold. In his hands was a huge library book.

"You sure have been quiet today, Lizzy," he said. "Did something happen at school?" Steven waited. When she did not respond, he handed her the book. "I checked this out of the library. It tells a lot about what Misaki went through."

Lizzy looked at the cover and turned the pages of black and white photographs. She stopped when she got to the page marked with a gum wrapper. A building of lava rock. Towers of wood. Men with rifles. A fence.

"There were so many difficult things about being at Minidoka," Steven said, as if he had heard her thoughts. "This page talks about the barbed-wire fence that was built after all the people moved in."

Reaching for the memory box, Lizzy opened the lid. She removed all the items until she came to the one at the bottom. A braid of metal. She gently felt the tip of the spike in the middle with her thumb.

Misaki. Her Misaki was made to live behind this mean, metal fence.

"This fence was very controversial," Steven continued. "Many did not think it was right, but our governor insisted it be built. There was just so much

Blossoms in the Desert

fear at the time. Japanese-Americans weren't trusted." He took the piece of barbed wire from her hands and spun it slowly in his own.

Lizzy studied the angles in the barb until it stopped moving.

Steven turned the page. "And this talks about how they had to fill out a paper. It was called the Loyalty Oath. Were they loyal to the United States or to the Emperor of Japan? But the questions were confusing, so many weren't sure how to answer them. It created a lot of worry. I have this book checked out for two weeks. We can look at it more later. Goodnight, Lizzy."

After her brother left the room, Elizabeth thought about fences. She read from the memoire, though she almost had it memorized.

Anger pushed down brews slowly. Ours had thickened. It flowed out of cracks in our resolve, like lava from a fissure. Surely our loyalty had been proven. We had never resisted. We had never fought back at the indecencies imposed upon us. We had

79

built a community in the desert and would work hard so that the land would produce. We would help America win the War. But the insult was a deep wound. Oh, why was it there? What were they so afraid of?

Arguments began. There were disagreements on what to do or not do about it. Meetings with authorities ended with only bitterness. Each day the barbed-wire fence scolded us—we were different, we did not belong, we were not to be trusted. And it got in the way.

Fear. Fear built fences.

Fences keep people in. Fences keep people out.

And they get in the way.

CHAPTER EIGHTEEN

Supplies were spread out on the back counter. Miss Simpson had given each student a class list. She said they could make their valentines the way they wanted, but the rule was that they must make a valentine for everyone.

"If you don't finish today, take them home, but be sure to bring them back for the party."

Lizzy loved art time. It was the one subject where the students were allowed to talk. As long as it wasn't louder than a whisper.

"So, Bobby, which girl's gonna get your special valentine this year?" she overheard Tommy whisper.

"Who says I'll have a special valentine?"

"I know you, Bobby Thompson. You'll make one a little nicer than the others and glue a big candy heart on it. You're a regular ladies' man."

The expected joke from Bobby never came. He just smiled and continued working.

"Hey Bobby, just in case you wanna know, my favorite color is purple," Wendy teased.

Lizzy wasn't sure how she felt about having to make valentines for boys. She wasn't sure how she felt about getting a valentine from a boy. And she wondered. Was it possible Bobby might pick her for his special valentine? There were girls prettier. Girls who talked more. And girls who could walk normally.

No. She should stop thinking about it.

Settling in at the kitchen table, Lizzy spread out the 32 valentines. All red hearts. All the same size. She had written her classmates' names and "Happy Valentines" on each. Three more to go.

Taking a large piece of pink construction paper, she folded it in half and cut the heart shape. Lizzy drew a single rose. She colored the stem dark green and the petals bright pink. "Miss Simpson, you're sweet," she wrote. She glued the white lace Mother had given her from the sewing cabinet all around the heart. Satisfied, she set it to the side to dry.

Then taking the purple paper, she made a heart addressed to Wendy. She wrote, "You're so fun.

You're so kind. A better friend I'll never find!" Lizzy taped a red sucker to the back.

Now the last one. She wondered if she should make it special. And if she did, what kind of valentine would a boy like?

Mother was at the stove stirring a pot of barbeque beans. "How are you coming on your valentines, Lizzy?"

"I'm almost finished," she answered.

"Supper will be soon. I'm putting the cornbread in the oven now. You'll need to put them away and set the table."

"I just have one more."

"You can make it after we eat."

During the meal, her brothers chattered on and on. It occurred to her that they were boys, so she listened closely. Baseball sign-ups. Baseball try-outs. How they would earn the money to pay the team fees. What position they wanted to play. Who they hoped would be on their team. And when would the weather ever clear up enough to practice.

She knew what she should do. Once the table was cleared, she began her final valentine. She cut a square from a tan piece of paper. On it she drew a wooden bat and a baseball. "Bobby, you're a hit with me!" she wrote in bold letters. Smiling, she buried it under the stack of valentines. She was ready for tomorrow.

The next morning, her happiness turned to doubt. She had thought that Bobby's valentine was perfect, but dread grew throughout the day. Now she wasn't so sure.

"Before we pass out our valentines, let's vote for the winners of the mailbox competition. I will hold up the top three and we'll vote by a raise of hands," Miss Simpson said.

Wendy was beaming. Her Waffles the Dog box was one of the three. She had used an empty oatmeal cannister for the body and put a head on top with floppy ears.

The slot was cut into the hanging-out tongue. "Puppy Love," she called it.

Tommy had made a spaceship for his mailbox. It looked like it came out of a *My Favorite Martian* episode.

The third one was made by the little brunette who sat in the first row. It was a genie's bottle trimmed in purple and pink lace. "Make a Wish, Valentine," it said.

"Raise your hand for the one you think is the most creative," Miss Simpson instructed. "Spaceship." She held up Tommy's box. Eleven boys raised their hands. "Now the Puppy." Eleven students, both boys and girls raised their hands. "Finally, Genie's Bottle." Eleven girls raised their hands.

Miss Simpson counted again. Eleven. Then with a puzzled look she asked, "Who has not voted?"

Bobby cleared his throat. "Me, Miss Simpson. Gee, they're all outta sight! I just couldn't make up my mind fast enough. But I'm ready now."

"Oh, Bobby... All right, we'll vote one more time. Everybody please vote for one. Spaceship," she pointed. "One, two, three...eleven." Miss Simpson looked Bobby's direction and hesitated. "Puppy Dog. One, two, three...eleven." Again she glanced his way, pausing longer this time. "Genie's Bottle. One, two, three...eleven."

This time she glared at Bobby until he shot his hand up dramatically. "Twelve!"

"Genie's Bottle is the winner. Let's congratulate Susan." Miss Simpson began the applause and the rest of the class joined. Bobby's hands moved the fastest. Wendy shrugged and then began to clap. Tommy sat with his arms crossed and didn't clap until Miss Simpson gave him the look.

Elizabeth's hands moved together slowly. She liked Genie's Bottle, but the overwhelming thought that she had made a big mistake occupied her mind.

"Class, you may deliver your valentines now. If you don't get them all passed out, you will need to finish at recess.

Elizabeth took the baseball valentine from the bottom of her pile and slipped it into her desk. She would need to pass out her valentines and make yet another red heart before recess was over.

"I'll help ya with yours when I'm finished," Wendy said as she passed by Lizzy's desk.

Dividing the stack of valentines, Lizzy left half on the desk. "Thanks, Wendy."

By the time Lizzy finished passing out the half in her hands, Wendy had delivered all of hers and the other half of Lizzy's. Lizzy sat down at her desk and reached inside for scissors and crayons. She couldn't find the baseball valentine.

"Lizzy, aren't you coming out to recess?" Wendy asked.

"Uh … I … I need to do something." Lizzy continued to search for the special valentine.

"Okay. Boy, that valentine you made for Bobby was neato! Ooo, la, la!"

Lizzy looked up in time to see Wendy's wink. "What … what do you mean?"

"The one with the bat and ball. I found it on the floor, so I put it in Bobby's box."

Lizzy slipped back into her chair, her face white. "No, Wendy. I didn't want to give him that one. I set it aside."

"Well, why did you make it then?"

"I don't know. I…I just…. Why didn't you check with me first?" Lizzy demanded.

"I was just trying to help!" Wendy replied, exasperated.

"Well sometimes you help too much!"

Wendy stared at her friend. Her eyes squinted together, as if she had been stung by a bee. She turned and walked away.

Lizzy laid her head down on her desk and closed her eyes. She thought about what Misaki had said.

In the slow-moving days of winter, two things grew: friendships and irritation.

Living so close to each other brought challenges of patience. Constant uncertainty brought frustration. To outsiders, we perhaps looked the same. But we had our own experiences and opinions and personalities. What made those dark days tolerable was learning to appreciate and care for one another. And learning to forgive.

The Valentine's party followed recess. Lizzy opened her valentines one at a time, but didn't read them. She concentrated on what was happening at Bobby's desk. Bobby's attention was on what was happening at Front-Row-Brunette's desk. Wendy quietly opened hers.

"Thank you for the valentine, Lizzy. I really like it," Wendy said softly. "I'm sorry I messed things up. I didn't know."

Lizzy sighed. "That's okay. I'm the one who messed up."

She watched as Bobby pulled out the tan valentine. Lizzy's heart sped up. He looked at the card for a while, then quickly folded it in half and slipped in into his pants pocket. He turned his attention toward the front row.

Tommy pointed. "Well look who got Bobby's special!" he said to the students in the back of the room. Giggles accompanied Front-Row-Brunette as she turned around and gave Bobby a smile. Bobby returned a smile. But it was only half of one.

Wendy turned to face Lizzy. "Gosh, Liz, I'm really sorry."

CHAPTER NINETEEN

Lizzy went to her room and shut the door. Setting four places on the floor for pretend tea—one for Buddy Bear, two for her dolls, and one for herself—she began to read her valentines. Most were in the shape of a heart and said the usual good-for-anyone things. Miss Simpson had written how she thought Lizzy was kind and creative.

When she reached for the card from Bobby, she could hear the thumping of her heart. It was a picture of a big drum and mallet. It read, "You strike the right note with me!" It filled her with joy.

But her favorite valentine was the drawing of two girls. One with curly red hair and one with straight blonde. "Thank you for being my very best friend. Love, Wendy."

Lizzy put the stack of valentines to the side. She reached for the memory box. Finding the old photograph, she showed it to Buddy Bear before setting it down.

Opening the book, she found the right place. She read aloud.

The War raged, and America needed all her people, even those of us imprisoned, to help. The irrigation canals were being dug. Plans for crops were being made. We determined to join other Americans in planting victory gardens. Some dared to dream about ornamental gardens. Beauty was needed.

It became clear that we would give up our young adults. With their loyalty written on paper and signed, they made preparations to leave. Michael enlisted in the army, and the girls found jobs back East. I wanted to hold tightly to my children, but knew I could not be selfish.

I borrowed the tea set from Akiko, and dressed in Ichiko's kimono. With the precious matcha we had left, I served my children ceremonial tea. On the floor. Next to the mural. In our quarters.

"It is difficult to leave," Michael said.

The girls, with heads bowed, nodded.

"God has given me family here. He will care for me," I replied. "My children, my American children, do not forget who you are. Do not forget Whose you are."

Afterward, I took a photograph with a camera borrowed from the camp's newspaper office. Seeing their faces would be a comfort during the lonely and worrisome times ahead.

Elizabeth picked up the photograph. A young man stood tall between two young women. Two young women who looked very much alike. And on the wall behind them, just off to the side, she could see part of a flowering tree.

CHAPTER TWENTY

Lizzy looked out the picture window. Ice had lost its grip on the limbs of the tree. The final drips had fallen. Across the valley she could see that the line of white on the foothills was higher up than yesterday.

She turned to look at the piano. Mother had started her on lessons again, but today she just didn't feel like practicing. She had grown tired of her library books. She didn't care to watch television.

Her younger brothers were off to baseball practice. Steven was studying. Father was working extra hours, and Mother was busy at her sewing machine.

Easter would be here before too long and matching dresses were planned for them to wear. Lizzy had seen the fabric. While she would prefer green, she was beginning not to mind pink as much as she once did.

Movement on the street in front of their yard caught her eye. A group of kids came walking by. One of the boys had a baseball bat slung over his shoulder. Bobby was there, banging his mitt against his leg as he walked along. And skipping to catch up with them was her curly red-headed friend. Lizzy moved behind the drapes, shrinking out of view.

She wanted so badly to be with them. She loved playing ball at recess last year. But that was before.

The group paraded down the street and turned just past the empty lot to head down the trail to the park below. If only she could move her body with the same confidence.

Lizzy went to her room to spend time with Misaki.

The snow melted. Then there was mud. Mud that clumped up on our shoes. Mud that would not let go. And Ichiko's grief clung to her soul. Spring could not come soon enough.

It did come. On Easter morning. The risen sun revealed fresh green across the landscape and cast a glow on the snowy peaks in the distance. The river had returned, just beyond the wires of the fence.

We walked to the hall where our church met, Ichiko in her kimono and I in the pink dress I had not worn since the first day. Sitting side by side, we read the Easter story from our Japanese Bibles and sang English hymns of resurrection. We gave thanks for the light that follows dark. After the final prayer, I looked into the face of my friend and saw that the pain lines had softened. We stepped out together. The ground had begun to dry.

Lizzy looked through what she was sure was the Bible. She could not read the Japanese writing. *Kanji* she learned it was called. But she never got tired of looking at the symbols. She wondered if it was possible for someone like her to learn to read it.

Her favorite story was coming, so she went back to the memoire.

Spring brought cultivation. We told ourselves to work diligently. There were many struggles to turn the desert into farm. "Gaman," we whispered. Persevere. And we did. But the ever-present barbed-wire fence would prove to be our greatest challenge.

One evening at supper, Ichiko whispered in my ear, "Meet me down by the baseball field an hour before sunset. I have invited the others. I have something to show you."

We gathered on a slope behind the backstop. The high school boys were taking batting practice. The sounds echoed through my memory. Oh, how my husband had loved the game!

Ichiko opened her bag and lifted the secret out. We all moved in for a closer look—our breathing quickened.

"Where did you get that?" Akiko asked in hushed voice.

"I borrowed it from the mechanic shop," she answered, her eyes meeting ours. "But I don't know if I can do it."

The cracks of bat-meeting-ball peppered the air.

"I will bring it tomorrow. Let us think about it, and then decide in the morning."

That night I debated with myself. What my friend proposed was risky, but I settled on the thought that we must do something about bad things. It was time for action.

The next morning, we gathered tools. With gloves on our hands and boushi on our heads, we looked at the barbed-wire fence.

We could walk around through the authorized gate as usual, or we could take the direct route to the potato field. Holding our silence, we considered the moment.

A red-winged blackbird sent his morning song to encourage.

Enough. Enough of this humiliation.

I turned to Ichiko and nodded. She opened her bag to reveal the tool. I pulled it out, and made a move toward the fence. The others quickly clustered around me, so that where one of us began and the other ended could not be known. We did not turn our heads to the left or to the right. We looked straight ahead.

Next to the fence, we stopped to listen. No buzzing. Akiko stretched out her hand and cautiously tapped it with her finger. No reaction. Holding the handles of the wire cutters, I tested it. Silence. Stillness.

We began. Taking turns, we started at the bottom, cutting just enough wire to make passage. Pulling the pieces out of the way, we crawled through, one at a time.

Standing altogether on the other side, we had arrived at our dignity.

We made our way into the field. We worked and worried. Yet no one came to punish or scold.

In the evening at supper time, there was much talk. Some anxious. Some defiant. Most determined. It was a quiet victory.

That night, I sat in front of my mural thinking about the War. It wounded without mercy. It stabbed at hearts. Its sword pierced deeply each time officers in dress uniform brought news of a boy fallen in battle. War had crumpled us up and threw us to the side. Windstorms of uncertainty brought fear. Anger gnawed at our insides.

I prayed for help to forgive. I prayed for peace.

He answered. "But for you who fear My name the sun of righteousness will rise with healing in its wings."

There is the healing that time brings. There is the healing that God gives.

My War was over.

CHAPTER TWENTY-ONE

Elizabeth's birthday came the following week. She wished it would be forgotten. She did not want a birthday she could not share.

The day was quiet and slow. Her mother's eyes were red. Her father's shoulders tense. Her brothers acted strangely.

Mother had made Lizzy's favorite meal: boiled hot dogs on buns, potato salad, and root beer floats for dessert. No cake. No candles. No one would have been able to sing.

After the meal, Steven brought in a present, wrapped in newsprint and with a card: To Lizzy, From Your Family. "Happy Birthday, Liz," he said. The rest of the family chimed in.

She opened the package and gasped.

"This gift comes with a promise from all of us. We promise to coach you and practice with you." Then changing his voice to sound like a sportscaster,

Steven added, "You'll be a Willie Mays before you know it!"

Slipping her left hand into the glove, she held it up for all to see. Her name, Elizabeth, was burned into the leather.

Each day after school someone in her family played catch with her in the backyard. But it was Steven who coached her. "Lizzy, put your feet apart, right foot back with all your weight on it. See if you can twist your body when you throw. Yes, yes. That will work. Maybe throw side-arm."

She learned to throw a baseball with a bad left leg. Fielding balls proved to be much more difficult. She could catch the ball if it were right at her, but when she had to move to get under it, she would lose her balance. Ground balls were even more difficult. Her left leg wouldn't bend quickly enough.

Just when she began to despair, Steven said, "It must be your destiny to be a pitcher." She practiced underhand tosses—arching the ball over home plate. Steven taught her how to spin the ball, and he taught her what types of pitches to throw and when.

Batting skills came next. Unable to put much weight on her left leg, she learned how to do a half swing. "Hey, that's just like a good bunt!" her brother cheered.

Finally came running the bases. Lizzy learned to lunge with the strong leg and drag the other, but it was slow and awkward. "Well, Liz, your team can have a pinch runner for you. The pros do it all the time."

Lizzy knew she could not move like her friends and classmates. She wondered if she would ever be included. After practices with her brothers, she would go to her room and remove the fan from the memory box. Opening it up, she would cool her face and read the part about baseball to build her determination.

Eighteen months from the Day of Infamy found us marking time in the camp. Our young men were fighting in Europe. The Honor Roll at the entrance grew each week. Someday the War would end, but who would be lost when it was all said and done?

We occupied ourselves with whatever we could to speed the days. Our block was hit hard by the baseball craze. The old men talked about it constantly, reading the newspapers for any tidbit of information. Children played ball at every recess and after school each day. The Hunt High School baseball team became a source of pride. Old women were devoted spectators. I, too, was a happy spectator. We sat watching games with traditional fans waving heat and flies away.

After school let out for summer, there was a lull in activity. Passes into town and work permits for neighboring farms gave glimpses into the outside world. A swimming hole was dug and filled with water from the canal, and this brought some relief from the heat and the boredom. But nothing took away the heaviness of being confined.

One evening, Akiko's son came to talk to us as we sat in the mess hall. He explained that he was a manager of a softball team. A league for ladies ages 40 and up—Seniors' Softball—was forming. He told us how his high school friends had a challenge going to see who could manage a team all the way to a championship.

"That sounds like fun," I said. "Who is on your team?"

He looked around the table. Heads quickly bowed.

Akiko laughed. Ichiko looked up and began to giggle behind her hand.

"How could this be possible?" I asked. "We have never played."

"I'll teach you. What do you say?"

"But we are not young," Ichiko said, amid nods of agreement and puzzled looks.

"That may be true," he replied, "but you are all very wise and beautiful."

And with his flattery, Akiko's son won our loyalty and earned for himself the name Coach.

We came faithfully, in clothing fit for gardening. Several wore boushi the first practice, but Coach said it would not do. We would need to find baseball caps.

We worked on batting skills. "Keep your elbow up," Coach would say. "Eye on the ball. Follow through." The language he used was as foreign to us as when we first learned English.

We worked on fielding. The mitts borrowed from the school were all too large for our hands, giving us extra difficulty.

"Watch the ball go into your glove," he instructed.

We were lucky if we could keep the glove on our hand.

"Get your body in front of the ball. Bend your knees. Bottoms down!"

Bottoms down? That caused us all to stop for a moment.

"Get under it," he continued.

We would end with what Coach called running the bases. "Always run as if you were headed home," he'd say. "This is how we will score points. You will be faster than all the others." We left each practice out of breath and very tired.

During the day we studied the game—learning the rules and strategies, reviewing and quizzing each other at meals and at work. After much discussion, we settled on our team name: Red Wings. And we began to wear our baseball caps while gardening.

Lizzy would always giggle when she came to that part.

The day of the first game arrived. We felt the twitter of excitement. Nervousness could be seen in Coach's eyes, but he put on his sunglasses and pulled his cap down.

It was a long game. Balls rolled between our legs, and balls fell to the ground. Throws were made too late or to the wrong places. And we swung at many high pitches. By the end, Coach's shoulders slumped and his jaw was tight. It had become clear that being wise and beautiful would not be enough.

At breakfast the next morning, we chewed on tiny bits of frustration and shame.

Akiko broke the silence. "We will get better." Heads slowly nodded. We would not *give up. Gaman. It was what we did. It was who we were.*

Lizzy wondered if it was who she was.

She practiced with her brothers until the day came when she took her baseball mitt to school.

CHAPTER TWENTY-TWO

Bobby was the first to notice. "Whatcha got there, Lizzy?"

What a silly thing to ask. He knew what it was. Everyone knew what it was.

Shyly, Lizzy held it up for him to see. Some of her classmates gathered around to look. "It was a gift from my family."

"Whatcha gonna do with that?" Wendy exclaimed as she stepped into the circle.

"I want to play ball at recess," Lizzy answered.

Looks were exchanged.

Wendy stared, astonished. "You can't play baseball, Lizzy. You know that. You've got a leg that doesn't work." Wendy's scolding was interrupted when Miss Simpson arrived to bring the class inside.

Lizzy's insides twisted with frustration, but she pushed her anger down.

She was the last one to get to the baseball field at first recess. The captains had just finished picking their teams, but the playground rules said that everyone who wanted to play would be allowed. Bobby's team was short one player, so he said Lizzy could be on his team.

"Ah, man, Bobby, whatcha doin'? She's crippled. Geez Louise!"

"Take short stop, Tommy, and shut your mouth," Bobby barked out.

He turned and looked Lizzy in the eyes. "You gotta help me out here. What position do you think you can play?"

"My brother taught me how to pitch."

"Nah, I'm gonna do the pitching. You head out to right," Bobby directed.

Lizzy limped out to the field, fearful that a ball might be hit her direction. At least she was on the team.

All the outs were made from the infield, until the third inning when a ball was hit between first and second. It rolled Lizzy's direction. By the time Lizzy arrived near the ball, the center fielder had run all the way over and tried to make a play at home. But it was too late. All the runners were safe.

The whistle blew before Lizzy had a chance to bat. She knew that her turn had been skipped anyway.

"Same teams, same places next recess!" someone called.

She arrived last to the line, in time to hear the argument.

"Bobby, this isn't working. It's like we have one less player. It's worse than that; it's like she's on their team!" Tommy's voice cut through the air.

"Come on, Tommy, knock it off," Bobby replied. "She's our classmate. We can't leave her out."

"Just 'cause you have a crush on her doesn't mean she has to be on our team!"

A wave of shame washed over her. The urge to shut out the world was strong. Elizabeth fought hard. She just had to be stronger.

Morning classes moved slowly. She marked time by keeping her mind busy. When Miss Simpson lined up the class for lunch, she knew what she should do.

Lizzy ate quickly and was the first at her table to finish.

"It was an accident," she said loudly.

Forks and milk cartons suspended in midair.

"I was hit by a truck—it's why my leg doesn't work." The questions she feared did not come. Only silence met the revelation.

"I really want to play ball. Bobby, I can pitch. Please."

Out in the field, Bobby gathered the team around him. He looked at Lizzy. "You sure?" Lizzy nodded.

"Okay." Bobby shrugged his shoulders. "Let's give it a try." Accompanied by Tommy's grumbles, Bobby called out commands to reposition the team. Then he took his place at second base. The game picked up in the fourth inning.

Lizzy threw pitches that were easy for the other team to hit. Pitches that were flat. Pitches right over the plate. The infielders had to cover her position because she couldn't move quickly enough.

Finally, the third out came and her team went in to bat. She knew she would be the last batter. With fingers laced in the chain-link fencing, she stood by herself behind the backstop. She watched her team score enough runs to tie up the game.

She made her way back to the field for the fifth inning. Finding her confidence, she began to get tricky with the pitches—deepening the arc, changing the speeds, and spinning the ball. Two outs.

Wendy came up to the plate, a bewildered look on her face. Tapping the bat on home plate and positioning herself, she brushed her red hair away from her face and turned her head toward her friend. Wendy's knuckles became white as she tightened the grip on the bat. The first pitch came in, and she swung furiously at the air.

Strike one.

She caught part of the second pitch and it went foul.

Strike two.

"Come on, Wendy. Get a hit!" someone behind the backstop yelled. "You can't let a cripple get you!"

Wendy backed away from the plate and stared in the direction of the loud mouth. The chatter stopped, and a hush fell over the baseball diamond.

Lizzy's eyes blinked hard.

Wendy stepped back into the batter's box. Both batter and pitcher took a deep breath.

The third pitch came in wide. Outside.

Ball one. Cheers erupted from behind the backstop.

"Come, on, Lizzy! You can do it, kid!" the boy on third base called out.

As the ball left Lizzy's hand, she knew it felt right. High arc. On target.

Wendy's back elbow was up, and she waited patiently for what was surely the perfect pitch. At the last moment, the ball spun off its path and to the outside. Wendy swung at air.

Lizzy's team cheered as the bell rang. "Far out!" Bobby yelled as the players ran to line up next to the building.

Wendy stood, still holding the bat.

Lizzy made her way to home plate. Without a word, she took the bat out of her friend's hands and leaned it up against the backstop.

Returning, she put her arm around Wendy's shoulder. They began the walk across the playground, side by side. When they neared the blacktop, they broke into a run—Wendy's smooth stride matched to Lizzy's hobble. Running brought smiles to their faces.

It truly was a perfect day to play.

That evening, Lizzy studied the walls of her bedroom. Mother had wanted to change the wallpaper, but she had come to love the pink roses. So, the walls had been carefully scrubbed and cleaned. Now they looked fresh and new, just like the green leaves and buds in the rose garden under the picture window. New life.

She took the blue ribbon out of the box. Its gold printing had faded, but she knew what it said. Today she felt as if the ribbon was her own. Opening Misaki's memoire, she read the final pages.

The new farm fields turned green and gave food. Food that would feed those of us in the camp. By the following year, the gardens and crops would be so abundant that our extras would be shipped to places in need. We were proud to have accomplished this together.

It was the same with the Red Wings. That summer, we worked hard, practicing every chance we had. The first time we won a game, Coach grinned and yelled, "You are wise and beautiful!"

He would not win the challenge that year, but the next year, we gave him the Sagebrush World Series trophy, just before he went off to basic. We knew he would be successful in the army. We had trained him well.

"Always run as if you are headed home," we told him.

Home. I had left my home in Japan as a young woman to fly on wings of hope. I had been plucked out of my Oregon home and dropped into a barren place. Yet, there I learned to be at home. And then one day, with a quick wind of Providence, it was over.

We were told to leave. As if we could blow away as easily as the tumbleweeds. Though we had proven our loyalty, we were not citizens. We were not allowed to own property.

The fields we worked would go to others, and the buildings we lived in would serve the livestock of local farmers. For many Issei, what was before the War was no more. We knew that our very faces on the outside would be unwelcomed reminders of the enemy.

But there was no choice, so with painful farewells and the twenty-five dollars we were given, we left. Our lives would have to begin again somewhere else.

Almost fifteen years have passed since leaving Minidoka. I am writing this as I sit in my beautiful home. Brick, not wood. Pink trim. Rose garden. Floral wallpaper. Warmth. Michael bought the house for me after the War and here I have found a good home.

I have learned that home is much more than a place. Home is where He is.

So, Dear One, if you ever find yourself drifting away from Goodness, run Home as fast as you can.

May His healing bring you peace.

CHAPTER TWENTY-THREE

Lizzy listened carefully. She always loved the singing at church, but the talking part was never interesting. This Sunday was different. The preacher seemed to be speaking just to her.

" 'Casting all your care upon Him, for He careth for you,' the Bible says. God loves you so much! Don't keep your problems to yourself. Don't hold your sorrow inside. Tell Him about it. He's there waiting to help. He will heal your hurts."

As the congregation sang the closing song, "What a Friend We Have in Jesus," Lizzy closed her eyes. "Help me Jesus," she prayed. Great sadness seeped into her heart as her memory returned. Details scrolled by in her mind. Vivid images appeared. And loss overwhelmed.

Oh, why did the Bad Day happen? Why did it take my sister away? I miss her so much!

The reality of it all sunk in. She wept. She felt her mother's arms around her and whispered prayers surrounded her. Grief poured out. Love poured in.

And she heard Him say, "Here I Am."

CHAPTER TWENTY-FOUR

The day of goodbye arrived on a Saturday in early June. Michael Sato parked his Rambler in front of the house. Though his steps were uneven, his stride was confident.

He was not a young man as she had pictured. Mother offered him iced tea and Father invited him to sit in his chair. Lizzy and her brothers sat quietly to listen to the conversation.

"My mother loved the beauty of nature," Michael began. "After she moved in, she planted the peace roses and built up the gardens until it seemed like something was always in bloom."

Beautiful Bloom, Lizzy thought, as she traced the carved blossoms with her fingers one final time.

Michael added, "I think she chose this house because of that flowering plum tree in the front yard. She always said that when it was time for her to go to her heavenly home that she'd fly away through its branches." The memory made him smile.

"Lizzy, it's time to give Mr. Sato the box," Father directed.

She had thought a lot about this moment. It was difficult to let go, but she knew she could not be selfish. Standing, she held the box in her two hands and presented it with a bow. Mr. Sato stood and bowed. Then he took it into his two hands.

"Thank you for taking such good care of it," he said with a shaky voice.

That afternoon, she went out into the front yard and sat for a while under the tree. She marveled at its strong limbs and how what had been white blossoms were becoming fruit. A gentle perfume filled her nostrils with pleasure.

It was time.

Lizzy reached up and grabbed the lower branch. With all her strength, she held her weight and pulled herself as both feet fought to find notches of support.

"You're almost there, Lizzy. Gaman. Don't give up," she told herself.

Pushing with the little help her left leg could offer, and pulling with her arms, one last surge of energy burst out of her. She landed her right leg into the crook where the trunk forked in two. She stretched to her full height, and then shinnied onto the biggest branch. Positioning herself, she sat in the comfort of the tree.

She looked at the mountains, greened by spring. She studied the town in the valley beneath. She looked at each house on her neighborhood street surrounded by trees of their own. Then she turned back to see the brick house. Misaki's home. Her home.

The view was somehow better from the tree. Her heart-smile bubbled up, and she giggled.

A mourning dove was startled by the sound. Elizabeth Farris watched it fly through the branches. Then gracing the sky, it disappeared.

EPILOGUE

The Honda Civic pulled over to the gravel shoulder. The woman with feathered blonde hair sat still for a while behind the wheel. Then pulling off her sunglasses, she strained to see through the harvest haze.

The entrance to Minidoka Relocation Camp was as she had imaged it would be. A structure made of black basalt rock. An empty canal. Yet she did not see much else. What farmers had not taken, the desert had reclaimed.

Grabbing her corduroy jacket, she pushed the car door against the October wind.

She observed the scenery in detail. The dried grasses. Seed pods on bushes. The profile of a rock outcrop. Mountains in the distance not yet dressed in white. A sea of brown. She knew this to be the landscape of her beginnings.

Fighting to steady emotions, she began to walk. A slight limp in her gait. She passed by barren slabs of concrete, discarded boards, and an old root cellar. She imagined the *bonsai* gardens in front of barracks and a game of baseball being played in a clearing below. As she walked along the bank of the canal, she spotted pieces of rusty metal. A chill shook her shoulders.

Had she not known Misaki's account by heart, she would never have believed this to have been home to thousands. Only the wind seemed to carry its memory. The camp. The prison. The place of internment. So many lives disrupted. Yet so much life lived here.

Then she thought about that day long ago. The accident that happened just about ten miles from this place. The devastation of losing her sister and how it changed so many things. Sitting down next to a clump of sagebrush, she bowed her head.

How is it possible that good can come from bad?

A woman she never met gave her comfort and courage. Her voice spoke Wisdom. There is the healing that time brings. There is the healing that God gives.

Yes, we must always remember.

Then she saw it. A low-lying thistle next to the tall bush. Pink. Deep pink. A pesky old weed in full bloom. Elizabeth laughed to see such unexpected beauty.

There truly are blossoms in the desert.

ABOUT THE AUTHOR

Debby L Wynkoop has always loved exploring the land and the history of Idaho. Upon completing a 34-year career teaching Idaho kids along with a 25-year stint performing southern gospel music, she is taking her "road not taken," weaving stories and composing poetry. She makes her home in Southwest Idaho with husband, Dave Johnson, and their cat, Sugar.

www.ingramcontent.com/pod-product-compliance
Lightning Source LLC
Chambersburg PA
CBHW021921170626

46807CB00007B/2924